DANGER
AT THE DIESELWORKS

Illustrated by Tommy Stubbs

A Random House PICTUREBACK® Book

Random House New York

Thomas the Tank Engine & Friends™

CREATED BY BRITT ALLCROFT

Based on The Railway Series by The Reverend W Awdry.

ISBN: 978-0-375-86799-6

www.randomhouse.com/kids   www.thomasandfriends.com

Printed in the United States of America   10 9 8 7 6 5 4 3

HIT entertainment

The sky over the Island of Sodor was usually calm and blue. But one day, as Thomas and Percy were enjoying a ride in the countryside, they saw black clouds of smoke. They knew there was a fire, and they raced to help.

An old farm shed was in flames. Thomas and Percy let the farmhands take buckets of water from their tanks. Luckily, a new engine named Belle arrived. She could shoot water from her tanks. The flames fizzled and went out.

Everybody agreed that Belle was a Really Useful Engine. Belle
was happy to help, but she knew Sodor needed a real fire engine.
"You need Flynn the Fire Engine. He's a real hero!" she peeped.
Sir Topham Hatt thought this was an excellent idea.

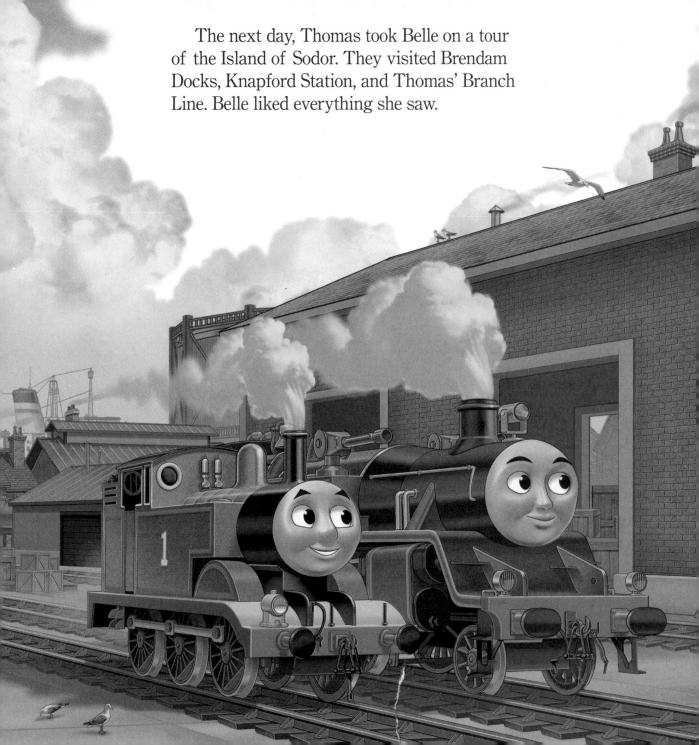

The next day, Thomas took Belle on a tour
of the Island of Sodor. They visited Brendam
Docks, Knapford Station, and Thomas' Branch
Line. Belle liked everything she saw.

Thomas and Belle didn't ask Percy to go with them on the tour. Diesel noticed that Percy was lonely and slid up next to him.

"Thomas is very busy with that new blue engine," Diesel hissed. He invited Percy to visit the Dieselworks.

Percy wasn't sure he should go to the Dieselworks.
Thomas always said Steamies shouldn't puff there—
but Thomas didn't seem to care about Percy lately.
Percy slowly rolled to the Dieselworks. His axles tingled.

"Hello, Percy!" boomed Diesel 10. "What an honor. Please come in."
The Dieselworks was dark, grimy, and a little scary, but the engines were all very nice, especially Den and Dart. They fixed the Diesels, but they didn't even have a crane!

"You should tell Sir Topham Hatt you need a new Dieselworks," puffed Percy.

"He doesn't listen to Diesels," said Diesel 10.

Percy had an idea. "I'll ask Thomas to tell Sir Topham Hatt. He always listens to Thomas."

Diesel 10 smiled.

When Percy returned to the Steamworks, he saw that Flynn the Fire Engine had arrived. Everyone was impressed by Flynn because he was bold and red and shiny. Percy felt very unimportant indeed.

Only Kevin listened to Percy's story. Kevin couldn't believe the Dieselworks didn't have a crane.
"Kevin, if you were there, you'd be a hero," Percy puffed. Kevin liked the idea of being a hero very much.

That night, when Percy returned to Tidmouth Sheds, he saw something that made his boiler bubble—Flynn was in *his* berth!

"If I'm not wanted here," Percy thought, "I'll go someplace where they do like me."

Percy found Kevin, and together they rolled to the
Dieselworks. They stayed there all night—something
no Steamie had ever done before.

Back at the Steamworks the next day, Percy told the steam engines where he had been. Everyone was shocked. Thomas' firebox fizzled.

Victor was angry that Kevin was still at the Dieselworks. He rattled off to tell Sir Topham Hatt.

Percy and Thomas raced to the Dieselworks. Thomas said he would help them get a new building. But Diesel 10 wasn't interested.

"Since Victor isn't at the Steamworks, we're going to take it over—and we want you to lead us, Percy!"

Percy proudly led the Diesels to the Steamworks, but when they got there, no one listened to him.

"The Steamworks is ours," roared Diesel 10. "And we're not giving it back!"

Worst of all, Diesel 10 said Thomas was being held prisoner at the Dieselworks.

Percy knew he'd made a terrible mistake. He quickly
went back to the Dieselworks, where Den and Dart were
holding Thomas. As Percy screeched to a stop, sparks from
his wheels started a fire! Now he had to save Thomas *and*
put out a fire!

Percy knew that only one engine could help him now. He raced to find Flynn the Fire Engine. Percy found him at the Sodor Search and Rescue Center. With pistons pumping, the two engines puffed to save Thomas.

At the Dieselworks, Percy convinced Den and Dart to release Thomas. All the engines watched as Flynn boldly pumped water onto the fire.

"Hooray for Flynn!" Thomas peeped.

"He's a real hero," Percy puffed.

The flames hissed and shrank and sputtered out.

Thomas and Percy collected all the Steamies and hurried to save the Steamworks. The Diesels refused to leave.

"Taking things and using trickery is wrong," Thomas peeped. "We can help you get a new Dieselworks, but you have to be fair with us."

Suddenly, Sir Topham Hatt arrived. He was very cross.

"Diesel 10," he said sternly. "You have caused confusion and delay. Because of you, none of my engines has been Really Useful."

Diesel 10 whimpered and his claw crumpled.

Sir Topham Hatt explained that the Diesels would get a new Dieselworks. "That was always my plan. Everything takes time. And everyone must wait their turn."

The Diesels and the Steamies agreed to work together to build the new Dieselworks.

When the new Dieselworks was completed, all the engines came together for the grand opening.

Sir Topham Hatt was very proud. "The new Dieselworks shows what can happen when all kinds of Really Useful engines work together," he said.

VICARSTOWN
DIESELWORKS

WELCOME
to the
DIESELWORKS

Everyone cheered and all the engines peeped proudly.
Percy and Thomas were especially happy. They were glad to
be best friends again. They giggled and jiggled and puffed
with joy.